Risk and Reward

My family has grown up around the River Doon and have enjoyed many walks and memorable days playing by the banks or paddling in the water.

'Mr. Goose' was quite a character who was very well known to the many people who enjoyed watching him and his curious behaviours. He was considered part of the extended swan family. Some locals think he may have thought he really was a swan. He would always be with the swans, honking and protecting them as he saw fit, especially when there were cygnets around.

This is a short story for both young and old with many layers to enjoy. It is hoped that it will prompt discussion about the importance of taking risks, whilst developing an understanding of personal resilience.

Our children and young people are growing up in a dynamic, complex and ever-changing world. Having the ability to embrace change and to absorb and adapt in a positive way is as important as ever. I wrote this story to convey the importance to my own children of understanding risk and resilience whilst also being aware of the impact they can have on others and their environment.

Thanks to my family and of course to Mr. Goose.
G.K

For my darling Cora.
L.McB

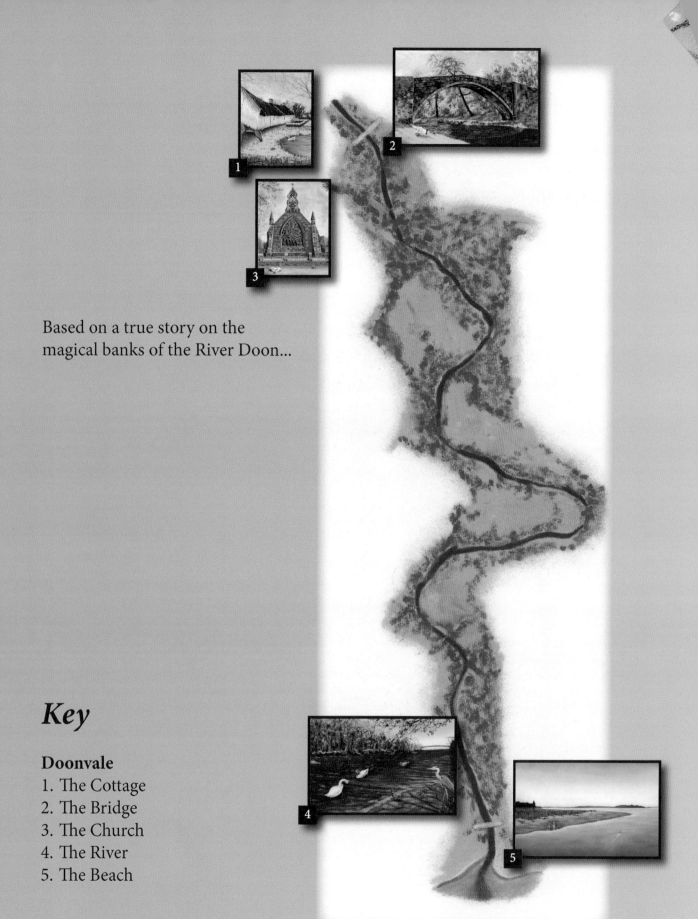

Based on a true story on the
magical banks of the River Doon...

Key

Doonvale
1. The Cottage
2. The Bridge
3. The Church
4. The River
5. The Beach

1

At the farm cottage, Mr. Goose was getting ready to go on an adventure...

"I'll miss you. Just listen to your heart."

2

Mr. Goose woke up one crisp spring morning with a spirit for adventure. He looked up at the bright blue sky and put on his scarf. He felt a flutter of excitement and apprehension as he thought of the day ahead...

Recently things had started to feel different and his perception of his home had changed. His old friend, Ned the horse, would soon be heading back out to the fields. Mr. Goose had been reflecting over the winter months as to what he wanted his future to be. He would really miss Ned, but he knew it was time to leave.

He also knew his journey was going to be long and hard with many threats! He felt vulnerable, but he was determined to go. He hoped to have the opportunity of meeting up with some old friends, or maybe meet some new ones along the way...

He would miss his morning swim, his daily gander along the pond and his familiar outlook. With one last deep breath, he looked at his reflection in the pond and remembered the time his parents had given him his special red scarf. The colours were bold and he hoped he would be too!

"Farewell Ned. You've always been here for me", said Mr. Goose.

Ned cleared his throat and replied, **"Mr. Goose, you're a great friend and I'll miss you. I'm certain you'll find what you're looking for on your adventure, just listen to your heart. You may be unable to fly, but you'll soon find your wings!"**

Mr. Goose ruffled his feathers, and stretched out his wings, wishing he could fly. Then he quickly got into his stride, waddling along on his new path. With each step it mattered less what route he was going; the important thing was his objective - **to find a new home.**

On and on he waddled, until the cottage and pond that had been his home and had seemed so large, suddenly looked like a spec in the distance, until he could no longer see it at all.

Mr. Goose is walking to find his new home...

"Don't look backwards, have no fear. Keep going!"

4

A breeze was behind him, gently nudging him through Doonvale, past a nursery, a park and little shops. There were other animals out and about too, but they all appeared to be going in the opposite direction. Mr. Goose nodded his head politely to them, still determined he was heading the right way.

A Little Mouse who was passing in the opposite direction scurried for cover - she had great foresight and had sensed danger approaching. All of a sudden there was a loud squawk from above - it was a hawk! He started to feel apprehensive and wondered if he should follow the other animals. He looked up and saw the hawk swooping down towards him. As it got closer, he recognised him. It was Hector Hawk, an old friend who occasionally flew over the farm looking for field mice.

"Hello Mr. Goose, is that you?" Hector landed softly on a Church fence and looked quizzically at Mr. Goose, and asked him **"Why are you away from the cottage?"**

Mr. Goose replied, **"Well, I've decided it's time for a change and I'm going on an adventure to pastures new!"**

Hector replied with some surprise, **"I thought you'd stay at the farm forever! You seemed very comfortable there! Where is it you're going?"**

"That way." replied Mr. Goose, gesturing with his beak with as much confidence as he could muster.

"Well, being a hawk I can scan the horizon and see far ahead. There's a river not too far away, but there's a storm coming so you had better be quick to find shelter. Good luck Mr. Goose, hopefully I will see you soon."

Little Mouse had overheard their conversation and hoped Mr. Goose's plans didn't go wrong and that he'd find what he was looking for. She whispered to Mr. Goose **"Don't look backwards, have no fear. Keep going!"**

Mr. Goose could hear some uplifting music coming from inside the Church. He stopped for a second to draw breath, gather his thoughts and gain that extra bit of inspiration needed to take another step along his journey.

Mr. Goose reaches the river and pauses, taking in his new environment...

6

Mr. Goose had been waddling for a long time and had become hungry. He spotted a bridge over a beautiful river and decided it looked like a good spot to have a rest. A couple of friendly children, Finlay and Violet, were standing on the bridge with their family, watching the water flow quickly underneath.

7

Mr. Goose jumped into the water, but no sooner had he relaxed, when a troop of ducks approached noisily...

"Oi, what are you doing here?"

Mr. Goose jumped into the shimmering water and liked the cooling effect on his tired body. He splashed some water over his head and immediately felt relaxed **"Ahh, peace and quiet..."**

This was to be short lived, as suddenly there was a loud commotion of quacking and splashing. A whole troop of noisy ducks appeared, as if from nowhere and were closing in quickly on Mr. Goose. It was difficult to count how many there were. One thing was for sure - they did not look happy at all!

The duck at the front of the formation, a green headed drake with a large body and beady black eyes spoke first, **"Oi, what are you doing here? Move off our river or there'll be trouble!"** Mr. Goose, who was still tired from his journey, blinked his eyes and looked at the army of ducks. A second, smaller brown duck with a bright yellow bill yelled, **"Yeah, clear off!"**

The lead duck quacks at Mr. Goose angrily...

"I'm not looking for any trouble. I'm just here to rest my weary body and be on my way."

"Move off our river or there'll be trouble!"

Mr. Goose wasn't about to be bullied by this gang of trouble makers, so he puffed out his chest, cleared his throat and said, **"Good afternoon Drake, I understand I may have just arrived and you don't know me, but I'm not looking for any trouble. I'm just here to rest my weary body and be on my way."**

Drake swam a little closer, backed up by his troop, and replied to Mr Goose, **"I'll be watching you."** As quickly as they had arrived, they paddled off, gossiping and quacking down the river.

Mr. Goose thought to himself, if only they could see themselves as others see them. Would they still behave in this way if **they** were in an unfamiliar environment? What gave them the right to talk in such a mean way to strangers? He could only think that he must have posed some sort of threat to them. Maybe like Mr. Goose, the ducks had their own fears to face!

Mr. Goose takes a much needed rest
on the island...

12

He was relieved that they had gone. He started to explore his surroundings, in need of finding somewhere safe to rest. Further down the river he noticed a small island close to the rapids, which looked the perfect place to rest. It was sheltered by a canopy of leaves and had tall grasses for camouflage.

It was getting late, so Mr. Goose clambered up the bank and made himself comfortable for the night.

Heavy rain began to fall relentlessly. The canopy of leaves that had been providing shelter was starting to become laden with water droplets and were beginning to land on Mr. Goose's head. Mr. Goose looked up into the night sky and shed a little tear, but wiped it away quickly. He hoped if anyone had noticed him, they would think the tear was just rainwater. He thought back to his sheltered and comfortable pond that now seemed so far away.

Mr. Goose quickly got on top of his emotions and settled back down to dream of what was ahead, but it was difficult to sleep because of the heavy rain. The river around the island was swelling and the nearby rapids were becoming more turbulent. It was not long until the river had risen up the banks of the island and was flowing very fast. He knew he had to keep his wits about him.

The storm is wild, and a little cygnet falls in the river and begins to drift away...

Out of the corner of his eye, Mr. Goose saw that he was sharing the island with a swan and her cygnets. There were six cygnets all together and they were becoming restless because of the weather.

The island was becoming muddy and slippery and the mother swan was finding it hard to keep all of the cygnets sheltered. The situation was becoming dangerous for the young swan family, as the water was speeding past them.

All of a sudden, one of the smallest cygnets fell into the water, just as the others were slipping in the mud. The mother swan frantically tried to grab the little cygnet, but the water was so fast that the little one was drifting away. The others were also getting close to the edge and the mother swan's attention was divided.

Mr. Goose had to react quickly and **honked** loudly to attract the mother swan's attention, but she was distracted by the emergency unfolding. He rushed across the island to help and honked loudly again. He felt piercing eyes upon him and noticed a fox on the far side of the bank surveying the situation. Mr. Goose quickly assessed that the fox would not be able to reach the rest of the cygnets and made the natural decision to continue on his mission to save the little one.

15

Brave Mr. Goose plunges in to rescue the cygnet...

Honk!

If Mr. Goose did not act swiftly, the cygnet would be swept away into the open sea.

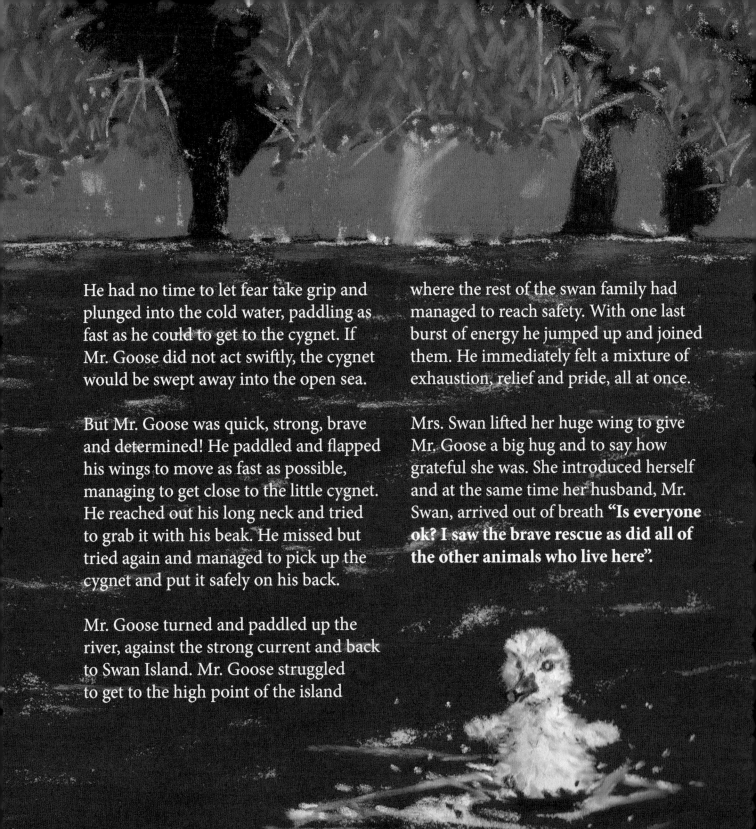

He had no time to let fear take grip and plunged into the cold water, paddling as fast as he could to get to the cygnet. If Mr. Goose did not act swiftly, the cygnet would be swept away into the open sea.

But Mr. Goose was quick, strong, brave and determined! He paddled and flapped his wings to move as fast as possible, managing to get close to the little cygnet. He reached out his long neck and tried to grab it with his beak. He missed but tried again and managed to pick up the cygnet and put it safely on his back.

Mr. Goose turned and paddled up the river, against the strong current and back to Swan Island. Mr. Goose struggled to get to the high point of the island where the rest of the swan family had managed to reach safety. With one last burst of energy he jumped up and joined them. He immediately felt a mixture of exhaustion, relief and pride, all at once.

Mrs. Swan lifted her huge wing to give Mr. Goose a big hug and to say how grateful she was. She introduced herself and at the same time her husband, Mr. Swan, arrived out of breath **"Is everyone ok? I saw the brave rescue as did all of the other animals who live here".**

All of the animals gather to thank Mr. Goose...

He proudly replied "I would be pleased to stay and look forward to being part of the river community with my new friends".

The rain had subsided and the morning sun was rising over the trees. Mr. Goose looked around and could see Miss Kingfisher, Madam Heron, Hector Hawk and the troop of ducks all looking on from different points on the bank.

Mr. Swan turned to Mr. Goose and said, **"You're a hero and you risked your life to save my family."**

"I am eternally grateful! You saved them and put your own wellbeing at risk - thank you! You're welcome to be part of the extended Swan family and make this beautiful river your home."

Mr. Goose looked around and heard applause erupting from everyone, even the troublesome ducks. Hector Hawk was so pleased that he spontaneously flew higher into the blue sky and circled around Mr. Goose, congratulating him. Mr. Goose knew he had found his new home...

Mr. Goose paddles to the mouth of the river to think about the adventure he has just had...

Later that day, Mr. Goose paddled down to the mouth of the river. He took some time to take in the beautiful view and reflect on the past few days. He was so pleased that he had taken the risk to go on his adventure and had proved to himself how resilient he was. Little did Mr. Goose know that he would live there for a long time and be involved in many more adventures...

Character's Profiles

There are many characters living on and around the river and like you and I, they all have different personalities. What character do you like the best? Can you write a profile for yourself or a friend?'

Name: Mr. Goose
Age: Early twenties (mature for his age).
History: Was looking for a new challenge so left his pond and settled down on the river by himself.
Profile: Purposeful
Genuine; mature, brave, determined, strong, protective, individual.
- Mr. Goose is an individual and survived on his own but needs to be an important part of the river community.
- He lets go of negative characters like Madam Heron.
- He expresses his feelings and opinions even when they are not popular.
- He is mature, confident and strong.
- He prefers meaningful conversations rather than gossip.
- Internally motivated.
- Makes the best of a situation.
- Doesn't get stressed or upset if someone doesn't like him.
- Above all he is resileint i.e. he can absorb and adapt.

N.B. He wears a Paisley pattern scarf.

Name: Hector Hawk
Age: Late teens
History: Recently settled around the river.
Profile: Instinctive and Irresistible
Loves life soaring in the sky, everything comes easy, makes an effort to look good, has perseverance and determination, very instinctive, likes to be alone.

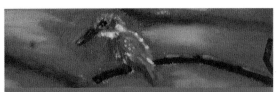

Name: Ms. Kingfisher
Age: Mid 30's
History: Always lived in the local area.
Profile: Easy Going
Very noble, 'royalty' of the riverbank. Can come across as aloof, though once you get to know her, very friendly. 'Still waters run deep'.

Name: Foxy
Age: Middle aged
History: A Nomad.
Profile: Toxic
Temperamental, a victim, self-absorbed, envious, manipulator, vacuous, draining, level-headed.

Name: Fudge the Dog
Age: 10
History: Lived in the city when she was a pup and moved to live in the house by the river with her loving family - including Finlay and Violet.
Profile: Temperamental
Loyal, smart, energetic, always fun, cute. Always on the lookout for her next snack or the nearest tennis ball. She loves her family.

23

Name: Swans - Rea, Geo & cygnets (one cygnet is a bit wild, always going in the wrong direction and not doing what their mum says).
Ages: Youngish couple
History: He has always lived on the river and she arrived last summer.
Profile: Alert
Influential, dynamic and enterprising, think for themselves (but consider others advice, especially from Mr. Goose), graciously disruptive, inspire conversation, proactive, respond rather than react, believe - always expect the best.

Name: Ned the Horse
Age: Old
History: Always lived in the field by the farm.
Profile: Cautious and Genuine
Not desperate for attention, doesn't show off, friendly, attentive and interested. Doesn't pass judgement, generous, treats everyone with respect, is not motivated by material things, trustworthy, thick skinned and is not a hypocrite.

Name: Madam Heron
Age: Middle aged
History: Came on holiday from France and decided to stay.
Profile: Enterprising
Sensitive; strong emotions and opinions, thinks deeply while waiting to catch fish, detail orientated, takes a while to reach a decision, emotionally reactive, takes criticism harshly, patient.

Name: 'Captain' Drake and troop of ducks
Age: Older
History: They have been the gang on the river since they were ducklings.
Profile: Temperamental
Boisterous, hostile and disruptive. Small minded and reluctant to step out of their comfort zone. They have wings, but don't use them.

Name: Little Mouse
Age: Youngish
History: Born nearby, moved away but now back living in the area. Likes safe quiet environments most of the time. Enjoys cheese and wine!
Profile: Cautious
Creative, inquisitive, empathetic, resourceful, determined and precise. Keen to follow the rules and talks things through.

Draw yourself on a risky adventure with Mr. Goose:
(Add in some new characters too!)

Publishing & Copyright Details

Original idea & written by: Grant Kennedy
Illustrated by: Louise McBride
Supported by: Margaret Kennedy

A Culzean Consulting Ltd product.

Developed in partnership with KRisk Ltd.

For more information on risk and resilience workshops for schools, visit:
www.krisk.co

Art by Louise McBride: Facebook@artbylouisemcbride

Design: TALL art design photography: tallwork@icloud.com 07788 447797

This book has been designed with two main age groups in mind. The bold text on the illustrations provides pre-school nursery children with a condensed version of the story. The main body of text provides children of all ages with an entertaining and educational experience.

Printed in Great Britain
by Amazon